The long way home

stable

Palace

Oasis

Desert

The Great River

The Christmas Horse and the Three Wise Men
© 2016 Isabelle Brent

For my husband Régis Félix Galand. Le petit livre de Félix!

All Biblical quotations are from the King James Version.

Wisdom Tales is an imprint of World Wisdom, Inc.

Library of Congress Cataloging-in-Publication Data
Names: Brent, Isabelle, author, illustrator.
Title: The Christmas horse and the three wise men / by Isabelle Brent.
Description: Bloomington, Indiana : Wisdom Tales, [2016] | Summary: Melchior's horse, Safanad, tells of the arduous journey he made with the three kings, who followed a star to worship the newborn king upon his birth in Bethlehem. Includes Gospel verses and historical notes. | Description based on print version record and CIP data provided by publisher; resource not viewed.
Identifiers: LCCN 2016021931 (print) | LCCN 2016013564 (ebook) | ISBN 9781937786625 (epub) | ISBN 9781937786618 (casebound : alk. paper)
Subjects: LCSH: Magi--Juvenile fiction. | CYAC: Magi--Fiction. | Voyages and travels--Fiction. | Horses--Fiction. | Jesus Christ--Nativity--Fiction.
Classification: LCC PZ7.1.B752 (print) | LCC PZ7.1.B752 Chr 2016 (ebook) | DDC [E]--dc23
LC record available at https://lccn.loc.gov/2016021931

Printed in China on acid-free paper.

Production Date: June 2016
Plant & Location: Printed by 1010 Printing International Ltd.,
Job/Batch#: TT16050402

For information address Wisdom Tales,
P.O. Box 2682, Bloomington, Indiana 47402-2682
www.wisdomtalespress.com

The Christmas Horse and the Three Wise Men

by Isabelle Brent

Wisdom Tales

"Now when Jesus was born . . . behold, there came wise men from the east" (Matthew 2:1).

My master is Melchior. He is a wise man. I, Safanad, am his favorite horse.

Many years ago a magnificent star appeared in the sky. It shone with dazzling brilliance. Melchior was puzzled by this. He sent messengers to his friends Caspar and Balthazar, asking them to come. They too were wise men of the east. I was excited to meet Caspar's camel, Gamali, and Balthazar's elephant, Simbalo.

Together the wise men sought the meaning of the star. The answer was written in the ancient scriptures. A star would lead them to a miracle—a newborn king of all creation. We would meet a child chosen to save the world!

The wise men made preparations to follow the star. They brought with them gifts of precious gold, divine frankincense, and sacred myrrh.

"Lo, the star, which they saw in the east, went before them. . ." (Matthew 2:9).

We began our journey, always following the star. As we passed through villages the people came and greeted our masters. They offered us fresh water and hay. The children would take turns to rub me down. They brushed my coat to a beautiful sheen.

One day a gentle breeze became a fierce wind! The sand was whipped up into a dreadful storm. Simbalo yelled to me, "Tuck your head behind my ear." With his body he shielded me from the sand. Gamali crouched down, his legs tucked in, his eyes and nostrils firmly closed. It was many hours before the storm passed.

Our quest for the infant king continued. We crossed mountains covered in snow. We descended into valleys of rock. "Step aside," Simbalo said. "Here it is my turn to help." Then he moved great boulders that blocked our path. Slowly we journeyed on, following the star.

At last we reached a river. The current was so strong, crossing seemed impossible. Our masters guided us along the bank. They hoped to find a quieter place to cross. As we turned away from the star, our path grew harder to see. I stumbled and fell to my knees. Melchior dismounted to tend to me. "You need rest," he whispered gently.

The next morning we continued on, but I was still too sore to carry my master. Soon we came across a rushing river! Simbalo put his giant foot in the water. The fast current was calmed. "Follow me," he cried. I feared we would have to swim. Instead, the river became shallow and the water soothed my sore legs. I could once again carry Melchior.

Next the star lead us to a sandy path. Hot desert sand! "Let my camel Gamali lead us across," Caspar declared. "The desert is his home."

All around us was sand. Sometimes we thought we saw caravans of camels and merchants in the distance. Balthazar cried out to them. No reply was ever returned. Then, just as suddenly as they appeared they disappeared. Caspar told the others that what we had seen was a mirage.

Many days passed. The sand was in our eyes and ears. It coated our tongues. "Do not despair," I said to my companions Simbalo and Gamali. "We shall find a way!" Eventually we arrived at an oasis. It was a beautiful place. Palm trees heavy with sweet fruit and water that was cool and fresh. I nibbled fresh grass and slept in the shadows of the date palms.

When we were rested we continued on our journey. Day and night we progressed, leaving the desert behind us. Our trail led us through more towns and villages. Then we came to a city with a fine palace. Our masters thought the newborn king might be there. But the star guided us to another place. Not a palace, but a humble stable.

"They saw the young child with Mary his mother, and fell down, and worshiped him: and when they had opened their treasures, they presented unto him gifts; gold, and frankincense, and myrrh" (Matthew 2:11).

A man greeted our masters at the door. Inside there was a soft glow and the smell of sweet hay. A mother knelt over her baby in a manger. They were surrounded by animals. Never had I felt such peace and tranquility. I bowed my head towards the holy child. My master Melchior presented his gift of gold. Balthazar followed with frankincense and Caspar with myrrh. But I knew we received the greatest gift of all.

"For unto us a child is born, unto us a son is given. . ." (Isaiah 9:16).

". . . And thou shalt call his name JESUS: for he shall save his people from their sins" (Matthew 2:21).

"They departed into their own country another way" (Matthew 2:12).

The children in the village greeted us goodbye. As we began our journey home, I saw the bright star slowly fade. It then vanished from the sky. Though nothing was said, each of us knew that we had witnessed a great miracle: the first Christmas.

Historical Note

One of the most beautiful and intriguing legends surrounding the birth of Jesus is surely that of the wise men and their gifts, which is commemorated each year by many Christians during the feast of Epiphany on January 6. These wise men—normally seen as three—are also known as the magi. In the Gospel's original Greek, *magoi* has several meanings: a member of the priestly class of astrologers and astronomers in ancient Persia; a magician; or one who had occult knowledge and understands dreams. Thus, the magi were probably Persian priest astrologers who could interpret the stars. In particular, the star that proclaimed the birth of the messiah!

Where did they come from and how did they travel? We are told in Matthew's Gospel (2:1-12) that they came from the east, but neither Matthew nor the other Evangelists give us further details. Over the centuries, artists and storytellers have presented them as hailing from different lands. According to an ancient and common interpretation found, for example, in Pseudo-Bede's *In Matthaei Evangelium Expositio* (10th century), each of the magi represents one of the three continents of the then-known world: Europe, Africa, and Asia. This interpretation, which I have followed here, continues up to today in various parts of the world, including Mexico and South America.

Although one now commonly sees the image of all three wise men mounted on camels, throughout history one or more of the wise men has been depicted as journeying on various animals—the horse, camel, and elephant being the most common. A lovely example of horses can be found in the medieval illuminated manuscript "Très Riches Heures" (15th century) by the Limbourg brothers. An impressive example of an elephant can be seen in the Renaissance Dutch painter Leonaert Bramer's "Journey of the

Three Magi to Bethlehem" (17th century). Examples of camels are also to be found in medieval paintings such as Giotto's fresco in the Arena Chapel (14th century). At times, the three animals are depicted together, such as in Giorgio Vasari's "Adoration of the Magi" (16th century).

There is much confusion surrounding the names and ages of the magi. Since Late Antiquity, the Western Christian tradition has generally used variants of the names Melchior, Balthazar, and Caspar (see, for example, the anonymous *Excerpta Latina Barbari*, translating a 5th century Greek chronicle). Also dating to that era, each of the three wise men has been seen as representing a different life-stage. The details vary, so I have selected Melchior as old, Balthazar as middle aged, and Caspar as young. They also represent the theological virtues of faith, hope, and charity. Symbolically they are the spring, summer, and autumn of life. They bear gifts of gold for a king, frankincense for a priest, and myrrh, a gift for one who would die.

This story is my interpretation of the journey of the magi, told from the point of view of Melchior's horse Safanad. Each wise man is described through his courageous and pure-hearted animal. Also included in the illustrations are birds connected through legend with the life and wisdom of Christ.

Why the name Safanad? According to John of Hildesheim, Melchior brought gold as his offering, including "all the ornaments that the Queen of Saba [Sheba] offered in Solomon's temple" (from *Historia Trium Regum*, 14th century). Now, it is said that the Queen of Sheba also gave King Solomon a horse named Safanad, which means "the pure one." What better name for a horse of my imagination who was to journey to where Jesus was born.

Snow covered mountains

Caravan

Valley of rock

Sand Storm

N